RIVERINE

Łukasz Drobnik

Cover Image: NASA

Edited by Janae Mancheski

ISBN: 978-1-952055-55-3

Cetacean

The beach, now a graveyard, stretches far below us against the background of the calm sea. Onlookers swarm around the place with cameras and mobile phones, all pointed at one spot. We're sitting on the cliff, on the drab flower-patterned blanket you hated so much, with a bag full of beers, having a picnic that must do for a wake. She's lying on a bed made of sand and brown seaweed and plastic washed ashore.

I've barely stayed in touch with T since I moved here. It's unfair, but I just didn't want to remember. I know he holds a grudge. I can see it in his eyes, in the hesitant movement of his strong hairy arm as he hands me another bottle, but he doesn't say a thing. It'll take a few beers more before he spits it out.

Now we laugh talking about you, about that day you decided to go back to jogging and bought those dreadful pink trainers to match your rain jacket. It rained ceaselessly that month. T scratches his thick beard and places his hand on his bulging black sweatshirt. He looks up at the cloudy sky and says it's going to rain.

A beachside necropsy supposedly revealed she was pregnant. Slit open, she rests on the sandy beach waiting for a flatbed lorry to take her to a landfill. T says it's always going to be this way. It'll never cease, not really. We'll just have to accept it as a part of our lives, learn to live with it somehow.

She's a sperm whale. Her grey skin reflects the sky, between towels left by those who thought she could be saved. She died within hours, reduced to what she is now: a rare tourist attraction in this somnolent village. T opens another bottle with his teeth, which always gives me the shivers. Then he resumes talking about a girl he's started seeing, who's lovely and whom I'm going to meet when I finally visit him.

They never found your body. Someone happened upon your shoe, the vividly pink trainer, a few miles downstream of our town. But that's it, as if you disintegrated in the cold running water, dissolved into foam. Dissolving into foam sounds much less dreadful than clutching at water plants, struggling for breath and feeling needles in your lungs.

I like to think you became that river, filling its channel from source to mouth, spreading further out to the bay, to the sea, to the ocean, wrapping the Earth with a thick mantle of water and now sending me this beached whale as a belated goodbye. Or perhaps you transformed into her. Maybe it's really you down there, heavily pregnant, opened up and covered in barnacles, with one fin broken and buried in the sand.

T gazes at me and smiles. He says he's missed me. Then he looks away and down at the beach, at the dozens of hands holding flashing phones, dozens of feet treading the sand and avoiding small puddles. He takes a gulp, puts the bottle down and holds out his hand to feel the first drops of rain. The lorry arrives.

Moths

The parking area is the colour of ash. We park a block away, anticipating turmoil. You walk in front of me with your head lowered, straight black hair tied in a ponytail, snow-white skin shiny with sweat. You glance at the cars full of shouting drivers, at the blazing sky, but you keep walking at a steady pace towards the trolleys, which are usually arranged in rows but now scattered in disarray. I know you're relieved to see there are some left. I know I am.

This time is worse than during the last January sale, when I didn't want to come but you insisted. It must have been a punishment for that dinner with my parents. Without turning back, you slightly wave your hand, as you always do, to tell me to grab a trolley. People swarm around, as noisy and disorderly as during that time in January, but the despair in their eyes has a new layer. We stop in front of the automatic door, and it opens.

The inside of the supermarket is a cacophony, sounds bouncing off its corrugated ceiling. Raised voices betray neither age nor gender, feet shuffle, plastic bags rustle, heavy boxes occasionally thump to the floor. At least it gives temporary relief from the unceasing heat.

We should have made a list. We always used to. That is, you always told me to write one and then, in the supermarket, you would give me orders: 'Take this', 'That way', 'Dairy first', scold me for choosing the wrong kind of blue cheese. I can't believe how happy I was. It's funny how we can sense happiness only by contrast, appreciate it only when it's gone.

Now it seems you don't have any plan. You look aimless wandering around the vegetable department, avoiding cabbage heads rolling on the floor, surrounded by almost-bare shelves still holding a few wilted carrots and Brussels sprouts, amid the restless crowd. *How many potatoes will we need? How many onions?* you seem to be thinking. Later, when you put bread into the trolley, your eyes look as bloodshot and helpless as when you said you were leaving.

We reach the dairy aisle. We revel in the chill from the refrigerators, our bodies bathed in the bluish glow. You no longer seem to care about the kind of cheese, not that there's much choice. A corporate-looking woman in her thirties prays while filling her trolley with camemberts and bries. We look at each other and let out a nervous laugh.

When you told me you were leaving, everything became distant. From miles away you said you were exhausted, said it wasn't working, said you couldn't handle it any longer, said you were sorry. You told me to move out by the end of the month. That was yesterday. This morning we heard the news.

We used to joke that we'd start drinking again only in our last days on Earth. It goes without saying now we'll drink ourselves to death, so as we approach the shelves once full of beers, the only thing we're concerned about is how many cans each of us will drink per day. We decide on twelve. I add five bottles of white wine, just in case. It's funny, I thought if we'd recovered from the drinking, we could recover from anything.

The ceaseless beeping of the tills makes me think of Morse code signals. I wonder why the cashiers are still working. Out of shock? Habit? Or maybe they were threatened? Before we stand in one of the winding, noisy queues, we take a detour to the pharmacy and grab three bottles of sleeping pills.

In the queue there are screams, there are quarrels, there is waiting, there is me looking at your white back covered with small moles, there is the slight shaking of your hand when you take out your wallet. When we finally walk out into the orange light, we raise our heads as if on command.

The Moth, that's what we called it, because of its brownish tint and clouds forming patterns reminiscent of a moth's wings. And the fact it is drawn to us like a moth to a flame. The media call it Nibiru, but we find that too much of a cliché. For now, it's a pale reddish dot hanging low above the roofs, barely visible in the twilight sky. We would surely miss it if it weren't for all the fuss.

As we're leaving the parking area with the trolley packed to the brim, I can't help but think our nickname isn't accurate after all. Soon it's going to be the other way around. In a few days, *we* will succumb to *its* gravitational pull, leaving the well-trodden path of our orbit, faster and faster, to finally plunge into the depths of those grey and brown clouds.

The streets are strangely calm. They smell of hot asphalt. Slowly, we reach our car, open the boot and begin to fill it with bread, cheese, vegetables, beer. We do what we'd never do in different circumstances. We leave the trolley on the side of the street. Before you push it down to the ditch, you give me a mischievous smile. We get into the car and drive away.

Devonian

'We need to go deeper,' she says, marching into the forest. It's quiet, as if we were underwater. The air is cool and moist. Ferns stretch their feathery leaves like lazy barnacles reaching out for plankton. Pine cones and pine needles crackle under our feet.

I can't believe we are doing this. She used to be so rational. At bedtime, she would tell us stories about evolution and mass extinctions, about oceans teeming with ammonites. Once she told us how the continents used to be a single landmass and, one day, they would collide again. My brother and I liked to imagine our beds as tectonic plates on a collision course. M sat on the Eurasian plate while I rode Australia.

We used to be embarrassed by her strong foreign accent when she came to get us from school. I still remember the taste of the greasy dumplings stuffed with mashed potatoes and cottage cheese that she would force on us at the bus stop, as if we'd been starved all day. Now I look at her grey hair and sunken chest and think maybe it's for the best. Perhaps she doesn't believe this will work either, but what do we have to lose?

We reach a small clearing. The air is much warmer here, dry and filled with buzzing insects. Small brown lizards hide under twigs and stones as we cross a sandy patch. We always knew better than to ask her about our father. She must have had her reasons to run away from him with two little boys, leaving her lab technician job to become a cleaner. Only once, when we got drunk together at M's birthday picnic on the beach outside our new town, did M ask her what he was like. Solemn and composed, she told us, 'He was a very charming and very selfish man.'

Her eyes are as tired and determined as on the day M died. My forty-year-old little brother lay there on a hospital bed hooked up to an IV, with skinny arms and sunken eye sockets, a pale memory of the person he used to be. He told us this state is nothing less than freedom. He held my hand and asked, 'Remember when I was Eurasia, and you were Australia?'

I wonder what the house will look like. We joked it would be a witch's hut, with a thatched roof and bundles of herbs hanging in the porch, but it might be a fancy villa built on hope. I can't be sure this is the right direction. She treads dauntlessly over the moss and sweeps away cobwebs with her cane, but I bet she's putting on a brave front. I wouldn't dare ask her how much further or whether she even knows where we're going.

Maybe we'll get attacked by a wild animal and die before we get there. Our bones will be cleaned of flesh by insects, worms, and small mammals. White and naked, our skeletons will sink deeper into the moss, under blankets of pine needles and autumn leaves, among the roots of generations of trees. Minerals from the soil might turn them to stone, buried deep under layers and layers of dust, with a kaleidoscope of forests and deserts and meadows and lakes high above on the surface. If members of a sentient race of robots excavate them millions of years from now, will they find the tumours on my mother's bones?

The forest gets denser and darker, the ferns ever wilder. It seems to have no end or beginning, stretching endlessly in all directions with its pines and spruces and birches, with groundcover sewn from moss and heather and studded with mushrooms. We can almost hear the distant murmur of tectonic plates.

As we go deeper into the belly of the forest, full of insatiable flora and relentless fauna, I imagine she holds me and strokes my head as if I were five again. I imagine she tells me she's going to be fine, she always is. If she survived our father, she can survive anything. Instead she just stops, looks around and says, 'We are lost.'

Cellulose

Days are seconds to her. Her stomata blink as she breathes. She enters through a broken window. She is welcomed by the musty smell of unmoving air and the old rug fluffy with mould, home to dust mites and parasol mushrooms.

There are no words for her springy shoots and resilient roots, not anymore. None of her numerous tendrils can be named. As she silently explodes in the living room, days and nights flash like a strobe light. Her chloroplasts are full and heavy, her offshoots ready to devour.

If there were a single pair of seeing eyes left in the world, they might find a certain beauty, even dignity, in her indifference as she tiptoes around the broken wine glasses. Gathers the scattered Scrabble pieces. Climbs the flat-screen TV. Spreads leaves over the sofa. Pushes a plastic eye out of a doll's head.

Calmly, she incorporates warm socks and bottles of expensive perfume and crime novels and kinky underwear and dry spruce needles and self-help books and wooden farm animals and electronic gadgets and bits of decorative paper and jewellery and emptied blister packs into the vibrant tangle of her growing body. As omnipresent as she is, though, she couldn't tell the dead Christmas tree from the dangling bones.

Slowly but steadily she engulfs the other rooms: the dim and humid bathroom, the spacious kitchen overlooking the green motorway, the two quiet bedrooms. It seems inevitable that her turgor pressure will eternally ensnare the furniture, that the rooms will be renamed after her vacuoles. If there were a single beating heart left in the world, it might find solace in the thought that the flowerpots, the empty aquarium, and the tiny ribcage will once again host life.

Meandering I

The river takes you with her, she doesn't ask questions, her waters aren't bothered if you're not up for a ride, her waters don't care if you're still bruised after that friendship, a friendship where a person who's supposed to be your friend is the first to notice you're falling for a boy, a friendship where she chooses to seduce that boy, where she fucks him in the next room, moans so you can hear it, a friendship that makes you think of razorblades and bridges and prescription vials and nooses and greedy seas, her waters, her waters lead you wherever they want, to this particular street at this particular time, though they could've easily led you elsewhere and elsewhen, her waters, like vines, trap you in this moment with sunlight and street dust and a bunch of people you look up to, her waters pour words into their mouths, they invite you to a pub, her waters swirl and eddy when you sit next to X, they make it clear X is your saviour in a stained tracksuit, a drunken saviour who's surprised you've never heard his name, who's a decade older than you and has a boyfriend, but the love between them has wilted, he says, her waters stir when X notices you're a tad unhappy, when he praises your Achilles tendons, makes compliments rain, her waters lead you out of the pub with his phone number, they know you'll be the first one to text, they're perfectly aware you feel more thrilled than guilty when X lies to his boyfriend to meet you at a pub and he drinks beer after beer and you get sloshed trying to keep up and when you puke outside, X is here with you and lays his hand on your shoulder with tenderness you've never known.

Elements

The night I quit drinking, I dreamt of looking for an open off-licence. All were closed. The snow tasted of ash. The neighbourhood stretched endlessly, blocks of flats and snow-covered lawns and deserted playgrounds. In that dream you followed me in silence, always at the edge of my vision. You smoked cigarette after cigarette, your lipstick left bloody traces on filter after filter.

The cramped rental car is filled with the smell of new upholstery and the quiet purr of the engine, barely audible among the growls and shrieks. Away from their husbands and adolescent children, J and K have let go of all their inhibitions. They're finishing off a second bottle of red wine, drinking from plastic cups. They ignore my remarks about the deposit, my complaints that white wine might've been a better choice. They sing our school song at the top of their lungs, replace random words with curses and find it hilarious.

They grow silent for an instant when we approach a long, windowless steel-structure chicken farm, built long after we lived here. As we enter the ghastly quiet village, I wonder what happened to the chickens. Probably nothing that wouldn't have happened to them anyway.

All doors are open. There's no point locking them anymore. We enter the garden through the rusty gate. It seems lifetimes have passed since J and I lived here as kids before she moved out to our grandma's. The garden is now littered with clothes, papers, and pieces of furniture left among the wild vegetation, a tangled living mass of weeds and bushes and garden flowers, bristling with pollinating grass stems and penetrating every nook.

Remember how, inspired by that cartoon, we would spend hours here saving the planet? We wore acrylic glass rings (freebies that came with a shampoo) pretending we had the powers of the elements at our whim. You were fire, of course. J chose wind. K, water. I, due to lack of numbers, had to be both earth and heart. (*What kind of element is that?*) Now it seems one of us would have to take over your fire.

I watch the empty street from my old room. Its walls are painted once-vivid pink, but the paint is flaking, uncovering the familiar blue. J smokes weed on the bunk bed, beige fabric hugging the curves of her body. The bedframe is the same faded pink, speckled with glittery princess and fairy stickers. She laughs and asks if I remember the hideous porcelain dog that used to sit on your doorstep. 'It's funny,' she says, 'we would shun you to talk girly stuff like making out with boys, when stories about boys were all you wanted to hear.' K enters the room, a new bottle of wine in her skinny hand, and says we should move on.

'Airlifted with injuries after crash.' Bad things that happen to popular weather forecasters always draw attention. I read the headline over and over, tried to call K, who wasn't answering (she shut herself off after that fire), managed to get through to J, but we mostly stayed silent.

The neighbours' gardens and houses. The pond, now overgrown with reeds. A deserted supermarket built in place of the playground where J's brother, my cousin, taught us how to smoke. The five-floor block of flats where K grew up. The school and the elm trees blown down by that gale. Finally, your home: the spacious villa of red brick, its roof lacking some tiles, some windows broken, the ceramic canine still proudly on the door-step.

I think about that time at uni when you and I lived together in that studio on the fifteenth floor overlooking countless blocks of flats, about that summer evening we spent on our tiny balcony drinking cheap wine, smoking, fantasising about our future careers as a writer and as an actress, laughing, saying no one could stop us, just let them try, flicking ash towards the distant ground.

Once they detonate the dam, it will take only minutes. The wall of concrete and water, dozens of metres high, will fall heavy on the valley, cascade down the fields and meadows, break fences and steal roofs, stretch above the village like a turbulent, translucent sky. The water will claim the houses room by room and stay there forever, make them home to perches and eels, transform furniture into bloated lumps of wood and fabric, eat away plaster, render wallpaper and carpet as delicate as a snail's skin. Before long, water plants will take over the streets.

Remember how, after you moved, we would call each other almost every day? You'd tell me about your disastrous castings and hatred for the new city, and I'd complain about my odd jobs, jerk boyfriends, and rejection letters. When we visited you at the hospital, half your body enclosed in a cast, it was almost as if we could talk like that again, as if we could save the planet one last time. That said, I wasn't too surprised with your reply when I invited you on our trip.

K snores in the backseat. J's drunken ramblings about her husband, that cheating bastard, grow less and less coherent until they fade into the sound of the engine. The darkening fields seem covered with grime. The sky is the colour of steel. When we drive past the chicken farm, I have this absurd feeling that you are here with us, watching us from above, gliding behind our tiny blue car like a buzzard.

Drones

Her fur is black like tar. She's hungry. When meowing failed, she jumped on the bed and climbed my bedsheet-wrapped body. Keenly aware that I am not asleep, she pats my sweaty forehead with the tip of her paw while I half-dream of guts and pearls and lost teeth and waves and robotic bees.

It always feels eerie waking in this place. Maybe it's the white carpets and custom-made furniture, the paintings, the coffee machine I could never afford. She purrs and rubs against my legs as I cut veal liver into thin slices. I leave her at her bowl, wash blood off my hands, then take my coffee and laptop and rest on the sofa. The Wi-Fi's down. Maybe they forgot to pay the bill.

I fell in love with your fields and valleys. While I clean out the litterbox, I recall the holiday we spent on that secluded beach, holding hands and drinking beer and looking at the waves. That was when you told me you'd never felt so safe. I pick up my phone to check my email, but the app fails to connect.

They were taking photos at the protest. Later, I saw some of the faces in the local newspaper. Banners above heads, mouths chanting, black umbrellas against the pouring rain. I felt relieved my face wasn't among them, then immediately ashamed to feel that way. Walking around the living room, I collect items from my list: the socks and the underwear, the charger, the toiletries, the jumper, the pepper spray I've never parted from since that late summer evening.

Calling you is not an option, not after last night. My only friends are on the road somewhere and lately I see them less than I see their cat. It's always been the simple things that separated us: the restaurant they liked that I found too fancy, the overseas travels, the meetings with an interior designer. Last night, when you woke me only to say you were leaving, completely drunk and furious and unwilling to explain, I remembered how hopeful we were when we moved to this city. They warned me the TV was broken, but I try to turn it on anyway.

I should have taken that job and left the country. It could've worked. I borrowed enough money, and the company offered me a place to stay for a month or two. Then you told me, as you always do, that you'd change and quit drinking, that we'd go to that beach again, revisit those fields and lakes and valleys, that you loved me and that, please, you couldn't live without me, and once again I believed you.

Why's there no radio in this flat? Radios always work. I put on my shoes, my coat, and my backpack. I make sure all taps and lights are off. I straighten the bedsheets. I stroke the cat goodbye. I grab the rubbish bag, take one last look around and leave. The key grates in the lock, and suddenly it's that late-summer night again.

They didn't use the word *faggots*; they hardly spoke. The shorter one asked you for a tissue, waving a fist with bleeding knuckles. Two twenty-year-olds in shorts and tight-fitting T-shirts, their muscles twitching, their faces now so blurry they could've been anyone. Guts like offal, bones like china. The crackle of joints and the stretching of tendons. Skin soon to be painted all over with bruises. We moved as if in a badly choreographed routine, taking the blows and losing teeth.

I leave the rubbish by the lift and go up to the roof terrace. The city is still. It's just stopped raining. I light a cigarette, surrounded by tenements, high-rises, and distant blocks of flats. It almost feels as if nothing's changed.

There's the steady sound of traffic, the squeal of gulls heading for the landfill, a ghost-like plastic bag flying above the roofs. The church bells start to ring.

I take a deep drag, waiting for the drones to come.

Nameless

It can see us from above as we try to hide in the bramble, hoping it will mistake our human shapes and movements for those of boar or deer or badgers. We freeze, blood dripping onto moss.

The Buzzard does a figure of eight against the cruel blue sky. The cloaking devices don't let it track us, but it still has its four camera eyes, motion sensors—who knows how many—and an automatic gun. It seems to have a mind of its own, and I can't shake the impression it knows all too well we have come back for our boy.

I can call it a Buzzard only inside my head. Perhaps you call it something else. Or maybe, after all those years together, we both came up with the same name due to its looming presence, the muted buzzing sound it produces, and the way it makes us feel like rodents in the fields. Finally, the Buzzard flies away. We wait a few tense seconds and dash towards a thicket of spruces.

It was right before his second birthday, when you were having an affair and I pretended not to notice. We were at home, just the two of us. He couldn't sleep because of a headache. I lulled his tiny warm body in my arms, unable to stop thinking of what you might be doing. That stupid lamp you bought projected blue birds over our heads, green trees all around us, slowly rotating in a dizzying loop. It was the only thing that could put him to sleep.

I look at the wound on your arm and try to tell you it's going to be okay, but all we can hear is a staccato of shattered syllables. If only there was a way to remove the implants. It's mind-blowing how we were so thrilled to have them put inside our heads. 'Just think of it', you said, 'we'll be able to understand any language, have the world's knowledge at our synapses.' But what we mostly used them for was liking stupid shit on other people's walls.

Now we can't even speak our mother tongue.

Clearings are the scariest, bogs the most treacherous, glens the deadliest. In places, the forest gapes mindlessly at the azure sky with its small lake-eyes of the same colour. There are innumerable pines and birches and spruces and occasional oaks, raspberry bushes and dense clumps of ferns. We are constantly looking up, arteries throbbing, freezing whenever we hear the barely audible buzz.

He looks as if he were asleep, save for the bullet hole in his head. Resting against the spiky mattress of pine needles, his red parka forms a vivid stain among the faded browns and greens. His lake-coloured eyes are fixed peacefully on the ruthless blue.

We scan the sky, then slowly spin our heads, turning our ears to catch the faintest of noises. I gesture at you to stay and make a break for the centre of the clearing. With wobbly legs, I kneel on the ground, shedding no tears, giving no sob, and take his cold tiny body in my arms.

You cry out. It's a mess of rustling sounds that could be reassembled into my name. An entire flock of Buzzards hover above my head.

Meandering II

The river takes you with her, she doesn't ask questions, her waters couldn't care less about your funny feelings, the way you're swept away when X tells you the news, turns out his boyfriend's leaving for a foreign country, how can he do that to him, he says, how dare he break his heart, their love not so wilted after all, you comfort him as he weeps, her waters wash away your doubts, with a little help from beer and wine and vodka and whisky and some gin, after X's boyfriend leaves, you spend most days and nights in X's cluttered place that his boyfriend is paying for, the two of you go out to pubs, walk the city's streets, get swarmed by restless insects near the city's river, her waters grab you and shake you and drag you through summer and autumn, in winter X visits his boyfriend in the foreign land, you think of lying down in a graveyard, your bones disintegrating, organs turning to puddles, cells leaking away, X comes back and announces he's leaving too, says he'll be joining his boyfriend in the foreign land, but hush, no need to despair, you should follow him, rent a place in the foreign city, find a job, make new friends, her waters embrace you as you cry through the night, they caress you as you weep out a slithering river, you seriously consider going, maybe it could work, X doesn't know the language, so you teach him every day, he gets irked when he stumbles on words, mixes up tenses, mispronounces vowels, her waters are relentless as they haul you to spring, X's boyfriend dumps him, so X doesn't leave after all, you're so happy you could burst, explode into diamonds, you both end up jobless, but you don't care, her waters don't care either, it's a scorching summer when you move in together to a place you can't afford, paint the walls white, the floor blue, it's not long before you take out your first loan, not long before you learn about his first affair, but for now it's just you and him within these white walls, on this blue floor, and her waters, her waters swallow you whole.

Deadlines

Your dear friend is in town, but all you've got is deadlines, deadlines, deadlines. She wears a blue dress and brings you ground coffee as a gift. The two of you have a blast, sure, walking down the boulevard, talking about your dreadful boyfriends, laughing, eating some charcoal ice cream, but there's a translation about bladder cancer waiting for you at home. You don't mind it, not really. How bodies work or fail has always fascinated you. Plus, being a medical translator means you get to translate all the ways you could die.

You spend the weekend at your parents', but all you've got is deadlines, deadlines, deadlines. Your sisters are here, and the three of you walk to the forest outside the village to hear pine cones crack under your feet, sweep away cobwebs with a stick. You cherish the moment, sure, but your head is filled with deadlines, deadlines, deadlines. And in the evening, in the living room, your dad sits inches away, flesh and bone, but each of you is submerged in a different reality oozing from an electronic screen. Your dad hovers above the mouthwatering green of a football field while you dissect a tumour.

They beat the shit out of you, but all you've got is deadlines, deadlines, deadlines. Your dear friend bombards you with messages. She wants to know if you are all right, does it hurt a lot, do you need anything. You appreciate it, sure, but at the same time find it a little annoying 'cause there are deadlines, deadlines, deadlines ahead of you and there are thousands of words to translate and you'll wade through them with your head thumping, your right eye swollen, until dawn comes and erases everything.

And all you've got is deadlines, deadlines, deadlines, it's always been the deadlines, deadlines, deadlines, don't bother me, I've deadlines, deadlines, deadlines, your life's a sum of deadlines, deadlines, deadlines.

Your dad dies of bladder cancer after he finally agreed to a cystectomy and even had a round of chemo. Your mum, your sisters, and you thought he was going to be okay and he did seem fine, and you didn't even need to call him that often, you were friendly with each other, sure, finally after all these years, and there seemed to be many years ahead, but then the results came in and it turned out the radiologist had made a mistake and Dad's belly was, in fact, full of pebble-like tumours and he kept losing weight, stone after stone, and weeks before it happened, he gave you his good earphones and now all you've got is

Airborne

Our cramped two-room flat is now a spaceship. You aren't here. Through the kitchen window, framed by those hideous maroon curtains we never got around to replacing, I watch a hot Jupiter devoured by its host star. It makes for a dramatic backdrop as I smoke a cigarette, exhaling clouds of smoke and flicking ash into that ashtray we stole from a pub. The tobacco company's logo is now barely visible on the scratched glass.

I wouldn't dare open the window. I feel a rush of excitement at the thought of all the forks and plates and ladles and unpaid bills—and me—being sucked out into the freezing void. I feel a pleasant tingling at the potential to join the spectacle of light and electricity and evaporating matter. The air becomes milky. I wonder how many more I can smoke before I stop seeing anything.

‡

Our cramped two-room flat is now the off-licence we used to visit night after night. You aren't here. It's only faceless people queueing in the entrance hall, unwilling to move when I try to reach the bathroom. Resigned, I join the queue, looking at our shoes littering the place, our coats hanging by the door, the beige down jacket you wore when you told me you'd been seeing someone else.

The unmoving queue leads to the kitchen where the cash register must be.

The walls are hollow, brightly lit with green LEDs, and filled top-to-bottom with bottles of cheap gin, the kind we drank night after night before I first got pregnant. I take two bottles from the wall, then two more.

‡

Our cramped two-room flat is now a submarine. You aren't here. The living room is drenched in a bluish glow. The livid light has two sources, the TV (where I watch a documentary on marine life) and the window (where I can watch marine life in the flesh).

I glance at the rug. The bloodstains are still here, although it was many years and many flats later, in my parents' house overlooking the white lake. The house where we settled, childless and happy, after they died in the crash. There was a blizzard outside. Numb and naked, I watched snow melt on the floor. You carried it on your shoes when you barged in, and now the two of you, best friends moments ago, scuffled among home appliances and designer vases.

The only way to find you is to go outside. It's the one thing I'm sure of as I stand inches from the window. A monstrous pink squid devours a hammerhead shark inside a jungle of brown seaweed alive with gauzy jellyfish. My breathing clouds the pane in ever-shorter intervals. Before I pull the handle, I whisper your name.

The wave knocks me down. My eyes are closed, but I can tell from the muffled sounds around me that the water instantly engulfs the living room, the entrance hall, and then, in one big rush, the bedroom, the kitchen, the bathroom. When I lift my eyelids, I am yards away from the flat, surrounded by a lifetime of floating toothbrushes and underwear and cotton buds, love notes and shopping lists that we would stick to the fridge. All I can see is a fuzzy crimson shape surrounded by a brown stain against a blue background. I try to swim to the surface, but the IV tube holds me back.

‡

You are here, of course. The room starts to take shape. Gone are the seaweed, the water, the tentacles. Enter the white light and the smell of chlorine and the tangle of tubes draining fluids from my body. As you hold my wrinkled hand, your steel blue eyes look into mine the way they did for those few scary minutes, years ago, among shrieks and dangling oxygen masks, thousands of feet above the boundless blue.

‡

Outside the grimy windows of our bedroom is an infinite stretch of wheat fields. I sit numb and naked on sheets with a maroon print showing the scenes from our life: lovemaking, quarrelling, boredom, pondering different options. Faceless people emerge from grey wheat, each holding an orange helium balloon. One by one, they approach the flat, attach the balloon and leave. Our cramped two-room flat will soon be ready to take off.

Spores

The superhero needs to save the city, but there's a drunk man eating a banana in her kitchen. The way he snaps off the stem and peels the whole thing in one brutal movement is all too familiar. She closes her eyes, just for a bit, and thinks of the cool forest air, her cheek against damp moss, his coarse hands under her blouse. When she lifts her eyelids, the banana peel lies on the stained blue tablecloth as lifeless as roadkill.

Outside, red-furred flying monkeys attack the supermarket. They grab trolleys from the car park and toss them at frightened customers, rows and rows of teeth rotating inside their black-hole mouths.

The superhero should be there protecting the little girl from abduction, the middle-aged cashier from being torn apart, but she knows the man wouldn't let her. The monkeys can see her from afar with their laser eyes, their shark teeth glistening in the dark. When the man tries to pull her closer, bits of banana flesh on his fingers, she instinctively recoils.

Later, they watch a medical drama, pretending nothing happened. He sits in the kneehole at his desk in front of his grimy laptop, drinking another beer straight from the can. She sits at his side, peeking at the screen from behind the yucca plants, a mini-jungle in this otherwise barren room. The superhero counts the man's beers. One more, and he'll get sentimental. He's just two or three away from waking the Beast inside him.

He drove her to the woods to take her mind off that boy. They walked over a floating mat covering a lake. Holding hands, they joked, 'You'd think it would feel more like a waterbed, but that one is pretty solid.' The layers of moss under their feet were the colour of surgical drapes.

They heard a sound like a bursting beach ball. Then another. And a few more. Through many punctures in the mat, with a horrendous, multiplied hiss, spouted plumes of red granular matter. The superhero ran as fast as she could among the erupting jets. She turned around to see the man was where she left him. He waved at her through the consuming clouds, completely oblivious to the hundreds of spores entering his mouth and nose and ears.

A rain of starving hearts fell from the sky. Clouds of capillaries shaped into force fields. Cardiomyocyte bombs. None of her many superpowers could save him.

The man chased after her, his eyes full of rage. Each step sent ripples through the mossy mat. The superhero reached the shore and ran into the trees, but now the whole forest was under the Beast's spell, every root and stem and insect at its ruthless command. A tangle of bramble that the Beast must have summoned trapped her legs like barbed wire. She only remembers falling through the cool air, her cheek smacking against the damp moss, his coarse hands lifting her from the ground.

The Beast's lifecycle is a complicated one. First there are the spores. Once they find themselves inside a human host, they form a mycelium that plants its roots deep in the brain and spinal cord, taking control of every neuron. This can last anywhere from days to years before it urges its host to hole up in a cellar or hollow tree trunk, curl up into a ball and disappear in an opalescent cocoon. Deadly vines sprout from the cocoon. They slither through the sewage system and underground car parks, feeding on rats and stray cats, leaving behind leathery fruits packed with slimy embryos. The fruits pop several months later to release swarms of murderous winged monkeys. After they've had enough human flesh, the monkeys dive into lakes or ponds or rivers, where they turn into furry, bloated, spore-producing bags.

The boy's heart looked like a frightened animal. She'd done this dozens of times before. Her movements were slow, steady, and precise. She never expected the bursting artery, the bloody deluge, the flatline.

The man keeps the Beast's spores in prescription vials, but she won't be fooled. The superhero has mastered the art of hiding them under her tongue. Before they have any chance to sprout, she walks to the kitchen, past the inebriated man, and hides them inside the banana peel. She dumps it all in the bin. On her way back, she glances at the gaping hole where the supermarket used to be. The monkeys feast on bones.

Meandering III

The river takes you with her, she doesn't ask questions, her waters pay no mind to wherever they take you, the two of you move to another city, in this city, X says, artists are respected, in this city he'll have no problem finding a job, but finding a job, he says, requires networking, and networking, in turn, requires going to pub after pub after pub, he goes out every day, her waters urge you to stay afloat, to take on new jobs, to take out loan after loan, the new city opens up before you, ready to be conquered, but you can't tell from behind your laptop's screen, her waters take you to the moment where X introduces you to Y, a first-year student in a sweatshirt who's a decade younger than you, X says it's only a distraction, a little bit of fun, but when the three of you go out to a pub, X introduces you and Y as husband number one and husband number two, her waters tug you along through month after month, X takes Y to a reading in your old city, introduces him to a bunch of people you look up to, shows Y the pub where you met, you'll never know what happened, but when X returns, he says Y won't be seeing you two anymore, years pass, you change places you can't afford for places you still can't afford only slightly less, X works odd jobs that never pay for his drinking, you max out your credit card, take out loan after loan after loan, but it's okay, her waters don't judge, you cling like a barnacle to that wilted love, a love that makes you think of razorblades and bridges and white pills and needles and greedy seas, her waters are forgiving, you get a job abroad, but X says he needs you here, not in a foreign land, he promises he'll change, you're dumb enough to believe him and decide to stay, her waters push you through years and years and years.

Landmines

It's a separate organism trapped in the innards of its parent. There's a whole lot of meiosis going on. As you point to the faded illustration with your bitten nail, I can't help but stare at your hairy wrist.

The pollen lands on the pistil. Just imagine, millions of beings encapsulated in these tiny specks, carried by the wind and insects and hoping they won't end up in puddles or chimneys or gutters. I move my head closer to the page to breathe in the sweat-infused air. Later that day, I play Minesweeper and feel the vaguest, most indefinable yearning.

We are drunk at high noon in the full sun. We can't wrap our heads around the beauty of the vegetation. I try not to think that you took me on this trip only to make me forget you are leaving. Two weeks of doing manly things like pissing in the woods and lighting fires and talking about all the girls you've slept with. Manly things like watching you undress. You show me the jar filled with swift water fleas, gelatinous hydras, deadly two-eyed flatworms. I wish I could also enclose this moment in a piece of glass.

We talk over the phone now and then as I drink my way through the angst of my twenties, the aimlessness of my thirties, the low-flame depression of my forties. Our phones become watches become chips become implants. Our hair becomes grey then thin then nonexistent. Fat creeps over our organs and under our skin. The pollen tube drills deeper into the cellulose flesh.

The road is wet and black, the stars are plenty. After hours of driving, I'm in your spacious living room on your expensive sofa, holding your trembling bald head against my chest. I wonder if the salt from your tears will leave flowery patterns on my shirt. When the worst crying is over, I talk nonsense to distract you. Just imagine, the pollen tube finally reaches the entrapped creature, one of the sperms fuses with the egg, and a whole new life begins.

Entrails

The night is moonless, the street empty. The air carries the faintest hint of spring. I'm walking home numbed by five beers, half-disappointed, half-relieved you won't be there.

Can't get that thing with A out of my head. What are we? Three consenting adults just having some fun? Two middle-aged queers scarring a nineteen-year-old for life? If A is nothing more than our fuck buddy, then why are you texting each other 'I love you'?

Tonight I'll dream about my father. He'll be dead, as he has been for a month in real life, but able to walk and speak and whine, wearing ornamental armour made of drain tubes and fluid-filled bags. He'll find the stash of beers in my room and pour them all away. Before he comes back downstairs to fall into a breathless sleep, he'll tell me to finally leave you.

I [will] [won't] listen to him. When you join me in bed at six in the morning, with your alcohol-soaked breath and heavy, fuzzy arm, I'll [pull away] [snuggle closer to your heart and liver and guts]. Tomorrow we'll have a fight. In the evening I'll tell you [to move out] [I'm sorry].

I'll [get sober] [keep on drinking]. I won't remember the names or faces of the guys I sleep with. In my memory, they'll become a hairy amalgam of legs, arms, mouths, and buttocks with many lungs breathing in the spicy scent of the cologne you gave me.

A will finally get bored with [you] [us]. [Your oesophagus will become a pipeline for beer and wine and vodka.] [You and I will really see each other for the first time in years.]

We'll go to A's funeral [separately] [together]. His mother will be roughly your age. She'll be standing still, her face almost emotionless, but I'll picture her on her knees, uttering guttural noises, sinking her dry, reddened hands into the dirt and throwing it into the grave. That day we'll have a [friendly chat] [deadly fight] and [go our separate ways] [you'll tell me you've been seeing someone else].

I'll hear about your [death] [wedding] months after the fact. The news will leave me numb. I will become a ghostlike figure haunting the city, feeling nothing as I get up, go to work, go shopping, until I break down in the middle of a supermarket for all the bloodless bank workers and heartbroken teachers to witness. I'll [go back to drinking] [drink even more].

I will meet [B] [you] by accident. You'll have been [dead] [divorced] for many years. Our dogs will sniff each other out under a weeping willow. The sun-filled meadow will be peppered with poppies, bristling with cornflowers. There'll be tangles and knots of earthworms under its surface. After my mother dies, we'll move into her house. Two happy, impotent drunks will sit on the porch, looking at the blue serpentine cutting the valley, holding hands, throwing sticks for the dogs to fetch.

[B] [You] will die, the dogs will die, I'll buy myself a cat. She'll lick my temple to wake me whenever I'm lying dead drunk on the floor in [his] [your] pyjamas. I'll learn all [his] [your] things by heart, exterminate all moths that dare to feed on [his] [your] clothes, keep a museum of bottles that have known [his] [your] lips. On my dying day, I'll remember your name.

Coal and Glitter

We'll take this land and make it gay, all its plains and rivers. The Vistula will turn gay, the Warta will turn gay, the Oder will become gayest of all. It'll wiggle its gay waters to Madonna at her gayest.

We will come out to you time and time again. Make you look away in disgust, pick at the many brims of your skirt with the multitude of your hands. We'll make you storm out, shattering the thousands of glazed doors. Give us a collective face slap. Hug us to your forever-sobbing chest and say you fear we'll be murdered in the streets. Some of us will.

We are the rainbow plague, the worst this land has suffered. Worse than town-slaughtering troops. Worse than child-raping priests. Worse than protester-strangling police. Worse even than neighbours setting a barn ablaze.

We'll sit you down and make you watch us in all our fabulousness, all the dykes and faggots and trannies of this land. We'll do a little lap dance if you behave, feed you a Tatra-sized serving of glitter-stuffed pierogi.

We will celebrate queer masses, give out queer communion, wrap every Madonna's head in a rainbow halo.

We'll come for your children. Make your daughters and sons alike throw flowers at a year-round pride parade. Teach your toddlers to masturbate, squash your infants into lube.

You'll never put the death camps back into service. We'll repurpose them as gay bars. Our army of drag queens will use the piles of clothes for their gowns, weave the hair into wigs. We'll karaoke our lungs away while prancing along the railway tracks. Put a disco ball in every gas chamber.

We'll take what never belonged to us. Shove the last of your coal up our fist-welcoming sphincters and crush it into diamonds. Make them rain down on the golden rye fields and smoke-spewing plants, the pine forests and landfills.

When there is nothing left but bedazzled wasteland, we will stop, the millions of us, and hold our hands in the open for the first time.

Meandering IV

The river takes you with her, she doesn't ask questions, her waters don't give a fuck about your father dying, X doesn't give a fuck either, a week after his death he introduces you to Z, a first-year student in a hoodie who's two decades younger than you, her waters engulf you as X praises Z's Achilles tendons, her waves submerge you as X says you need distraction from your grief, at this point you know what X is capable of, so you draw a line, assert you don't want anything romantic, X says sure, fine, but at the same time bombards Z with romantic texts, it's winter, it's freezing, not long after Christmas, her waters push you around the city's decorated streets, it's not long before Z practically moves in, X fucks him in the next room, moans so you can hear it, you take long walks not to be there, wade through your grief as if through a forest thick with ferns and bramble and moss, walk barefoot over pine needles, pop out to the off-licence day after day to drink beer after beer after beer, think of turning to bones, to ashes, of your dead father's tumours, of cells packed with vacuoles, her waters shake you out of your torpor and you realise something in Z's smile reminds you of that boy you fell for years and years ago, his gentle blue eyes remind you of small lakes, you realise Z keeps up with your drinking, so you dial it down, her waters, her waters, her waters swell when it's just you and Z sitting on the balcony, surrounded by petunias, nasturtiums, and cornflowers you compulsively planted, and you look into Z's eyes and say that you love him and, funny thing, he loves you back, her waters push forwards, X drinks beer after beer after beer, he gets irked you haven't forgiven him in the timeframe he envisioned, more and more often he bursts into drunken tirades, you love to wallow in misery, he says, you're vindictive, you always paint yourself as a saint, more and more often you sit in the dark kitchen in the middle of the night thinking of an escape.

Scattered

The watering can that gave you blisters

A photo from your wedding day that the two of you hung in the vestibule for all the guests to see

An empty whisky bottle, one of many

The portable heater you bought during your first winter together when it snowed all the time, when the windows were covered with ice flowers

One of the countless DVDs you watched on your old player when she was out with her friends and you were too tired to join them

A shoe cabinet you moved to the bedroom when there was no room left in the vestibule

The celadon sponge with which you rubbed her mole-covered back when you showered together in your tiny bathroom (the tiles were as white as his teeth)

A heavy ceramic pot, must be the one in which she gave you that small spruce for your first anniversary when you both started to realise the fifteen-year gap would haunt you later but chased that thought away and went on to plant the spruce outside your bedroom window so you could watch your love grow

The shears you bought when the clippers weren't enough

A dusty kettlebell, the one she gave you for your fortieth, and you took it as an insult

A pair of slippers you gave him when he started coming every day to help you with the unruly vegetation

The insecticide you foolishly bought when you woke up to find the leaves covered in a fine, opalescent web, not knowing that red spider mites aren't insects, you idiot

An empty bottle of rye vodka, could be the one he brought when he came to discuss the rules

Her blackberry-flavoured lip balm you found behind the toppled chest of drawers and applied on some of the bigger tears in the cuticle

A positive pregnancy test, broken in half

A queen of hearts, must be from the deck he brought to distract you on that terrible, terrible day when the two of you played drinking games late into the night in the verdure-filled kitchen

The bottle of wine you downed in one go after you told her to choose

A flask of her favourite perfume, could be a gift from you or him, or she bought it herself, it's hard to tell now, or maybe it's one of those you got after you-know-what to give the leaves that familiar earthy smell

One of many beer crates you used to sit on when tending to the vines, which he would bring you every week filled with non-alcoholic beers to help you out of your drunkenness

An Amazon-green marker, one of those she used for the comic book about talking coniferous trees she never got to finish

The electric bush trimmer you bought when it was too much for the shears to handle

Never-worn baby shoes

Her old phone, filled with love texts he sent her and she was reckless enough not to delete

The axe with which you mutilated the spruce after you caught them fucking and realised you couldn't compete with his strong forearms, impeccable smile, and unwrinkled forehead

A bigger axe you used to chop through the anaconda-like stems when they trapped you inside the bedroom

A pack of soaked cotton pads you couldn't bring yourself to throw away and watched during many lonely showers in that micro-jungle of a bathroom and imagined them as a stack of budding jellyfish about to break away and float up, up, up to the cloudy sky

The postcard from the seaside in which he wrote he'd met a girl and wouldn't be able to help you with the vines anymore and hoped you understood, and you did

A prescription vial, the one she emptied in one gulp and washed the pills down with some of your whisky and you saw all of that from the outside while tending to the spruce and it took you some time to realise what was going on, or maybe you knew from the beginning but just couldn't move, like the way you're paralysed when witnessing a car crash, and when you stormed into the living room, still holding your clippers, she was on a chair, pale and lifeless, her hair tied in a ponytail to expose a throbbing neck, and before you could reach her, she erupted into a ball of wriggling vines and leaves and buds and tendrils, sank between the floorboards with her many roots, penetrated the concrete and went deeper into the squishy soil to populate it with a myriad of tubers, and you couldn't budge, the clippers now one with your body, and watched her shoots engulf the chair and the table and the bookshelf and you knew that the vines would eventually extend into the bedroom, kitchen, and bathroom, slither into the vestibule and burst out to the garden, then roll down the hill and branch all over the town, feed on the dead in the graveyard, trap the living in their homes, you knew all of that but you stayed anyway—her vines entwining your legs, forming a noose around your neck—and watched the breath-stealing explosion

Phagocytosis

I wake you up from a sparkless dream with signals I never knew I was sending. They reach you, a frozen soldier, through the cloudy wall. The world throbs. Cells make a rubbery sound as you squeeze out of the capillary. I stand in awe of your doggedness.

You're so good at sensing my next step. You, you bloodhound, you. It doesn't trouble me. Even worse, I lure you in. Drop after drop, you lick up the bits of my cellular wall. I start to forget I put up this wall for a reason.

And here you are, shiny and enormous in billowing armour, so unthinkable and yet so close. I almost bow and address you as 'Your Translucency' while you inch in.

We just click. The rugged projections on our surfaces zip up into a seamless whole, as if always meant for each other. You open your pseudopodia so wide and inviting that I can't help but cry a giddy 'yes!'

It's nice and cosy inside you. In fact, cosier by the second. The world blurs. It seems I have lived here forever. Through your viscosity approach your welcome squad, at first mere dozens of shimmering points, quickly sharpening into opaque sacs. At this point I don't suspect they are filled with poison.

Take a bite, and I'll turn to shards.

Riverweed

There's a story in this series of vomit stains on the pavement. The first attack must have been strong and short, leaving long radial streaks on the flagstones. The second splash is smaller. Whoever left it must have thought the worst was behind them. The last one is an unrestrained cacophony of colours and textures, as if an artist held on to the corner while a jet of paint erupted from their body, hit the pavement, and cascaded over the curb onto the asphalt.

You picture a river similar to the one you used to go to with E before she moved to another city, before you moved to another city, but wilder, louder, and more beckoning. Its banks are flanked by weeping willows and bristling with reeds, its heart the blackest maelstrom. The swoosh reminds you of the patter of his urine against the floorboards in the middle of the living room, in the middle of the night. The air smells of river sludge and frail waterweeds and empty snail shells. You wonder if a person retains their sense of smell underwater.

The bruises on the thirty-year-old man's skin tell a story of their own. The oldest have wilted into soft yellows, the newer ones bloom with purples and blues. Some are mere seeds awaiting their time to blossom: the faint knuckle-shaped stains under the collarbone, the ghostly powder pink mark around the forearm. Loud snoring and the stench of vodka come from the adjacent room. A burly fortyish man lies half-buried under a duvet, his underwear damp with urine, bits of vomit glistening in his beard.

The rippling surface hypnotises you. You don't even notice the fluffy Pomeranian-shaped clouds above your head or feel the vibrations of ringworms and insects under your bare feet. If E were here, she would drag you to safety as she has tried to do with Silesian stubbornness in her many annoying phone calls. Once you dip your toe in the cold bottle green, you remember the psychobabble she spewed at you, her hair full of swirls and eddies, in that blue café overlooking the river. The machine-gun series of 'co-dependencies' and 'over-responsibilities' bounced off your skin as you calmly watched the waters roll.

All the fingerprints on the mirror won't shut up either. The medicine cabinet filled with prescription vials (*take the pills, take the pills*) reflects the empty white bathroom, superimposed with greasy impressions of papillary lines. Each print reminds one of a small lake, brought to life by the hesitant touch of a finger (*take the pills, take the pills*), the oily isobaths stepping down to the bottom.

Waist-deep in the water, you imagine you'll feel like a blood cell pushed by the turbulent plasma, a joyride up the aorta, if blood cells feel anything at all. Part of you, larger with each second, longs for this not-feeling, not having to lie in bed pretending you're asleep and wait until the click of the lock betrays the level of his drunkenness. Another part recalls that June night when together you sneaked onto the roof of your tower block and kissed for all of the galaxy to witness.

Words turned into electricity and back into words again don't leave much room for interpretation. The bruised man sits in seaweed-patterned briefs on a kitchen chair and whispers into a phone. When he listens, words seem to fall out of the speaker and stick to the stuffy air, forming a constellation: 'you' is just lightyears away from 'have to', but 'escape' lies at the edge of his universe.

Your head and the rest of your body now belong to two different worlds, cut at the neck by the aqueous boundary. Paralysed, you wait for the viscous current to help you off the slippery stones.

The exuberant kelp of a vomit stain is now sliced through by two wobbly lines like the tracks of small wheels. Could it have been the bruised thirty-year-old's suitcase? The tracks vanish in the middle of the street. It cannot be ruled out that the battered man, if indeed it was him, became a Slavic god by the name of Diazepamir (*his many arms forever toasting shots of rye vodka, lungs choked with catkins*), then soared to the night sky (*countless hands plucking tenements, tearing off asphalt*) and disappeared in a flash (*take the streets, take the streets*) where there is no fear and there is no death and everything is light.

Meandering V

The river takes you with her, she doesn't ask questions, her waters are unimpressed when you decide to move out, her waters swoosh around when you walk about a supermarket filling your trolley with plates, cutlery, toiletries, towels, when you sign the lease and get the keys, it's only then that you tell X, Z has known about your moving all along, X takes it as an insult, as he does most things, storms out of the balcony filled with a new set of petunias, nasturtiums, and cornflowers, their cells stiff with cellulose, thirsty vascular bundles, you move out within days, X bombards Z with texts, tells him it's over between them, he might as well end it all, threatens he'll turn to bones, to ashes, jump off the nearest bridge, X turns his many friends into flying monkeys, but you're smart enough to ignore their calls, when X sees his tricks aren't working, he proceeds to plan B, invites you to a pub, apologises for his behaviour, I love you so much, he says, I promise I'll change, but you're smart enough not to believe him, months pass, her waters flow, you dream of landfills, marshlands, quicksands, pay instalment after instalment, it'll take years and years to pay off your debt, you don't have it in you to leave X, her waters don't judge, you barely see each other, though, as X spends most evenings out drinking beer after beer, smoking cigarette after cigarette, flirting with boy after boy after boy, and you, on the other hand, spend most evenings with Z, the river's countless arms enmesh the two of you as you watch TV, as you kiss his foot and dream one day you'll get away, just you and Z, to traverse pine forests and rye fields, visit rainy jungles and secluded beaches, cross rivers and lakes and glittery seas, hold each other's hands, say each other's names until her waters, her waters turn you to ashes, to coal.

Echoes

So sudden you didn't have time to put your hair on. So loud your eardrums hurt. Who are these people who have stormed into your kitchen? Why does the woman loot your cupboards, why does the man produce a knife?

The woman's voice reminds you of your daughter's, but your daughter is five and cuts her doll's hair. You bought it yesterday, it cost half your wage, so you tear it out of her small hands (polyester flying), shut the door and weep.

The man sinks his knife into a chocolate cake that has materialised on stained oilcloth next to dirty glasses, a bunch of wilted fuchsias, your teeth you just realise you forgot to put in.

The cake bleeds, and you think of the river of blood you and your twin sister swam in. It was summer, it was yesterday, the two of you barely born, inseparable, immortal.

Vacuoles

Your heart, a simulation within a simulation within a simulation. Your hands unpacking shopping bags as they're meant to. The tablecloth; always plastic, always stained, always waiting. The sigh you breathe before you begin. And here they go: the cheese, the baby greens, the onions. The tasteless puffy bread he likes. And the beer, don't forget the beer, great men need to have their beer.

The chives, the peppermint, the beetroot. The swirling Romanesco broccoli, with that glitch in the fractal-making of its flowers. The mezzanine on which the two of you fucked, all trembling, on that bright January day. The lab, all those years ago. The deadly amoeba that engulfed a bacterium and called it a day. His phenol-smelling coat when he briefly put his hand on your shoulder and carried on teaching about tiny hollow spaces in every living cell.

The cocoa powder. The alphabet pasta that will never spell your name. *Just wait*, you keep telling yourself, after his birthday, your crystal anniversary, his father's funeral. *Just wait and see*, maybe this time he's changed for good. The brown sugar. The lemons. All the appointments he's about to miss. The loneliness. The many sleepless nights. And the years that go by.

Your life, a loop after a loop after a loop. Your hands unpacking new supplies, always the same items. The tablecloth, the waiting. The sigh you breathe before you begin. And here they go: the cheese, the baby greens, the onions. The puffy abomination of a loaf of bread. And the beer, more and more beer, great men need to sail their seas of beer.

The chives, the peppermint, the beetroot. The arteriovenous malformation in his head, that glitch in the fractal-making of his vessels. The mezzanine on which the two of you fucked, all jumpy, that bright January day. The amoebic cells torn apart by centrifugal force, their organelles neatly sorted. Could mitochondria be called a cell's many hearts? The sterile white around you when the other students left, and he told you he was leaving his wife for you.

The wine he likes to drink at lunch when his hepatocytes are not having it. The brown sugar. The lemons. *Just wait*, you keep telling yourself, after you've paid off the flat, after winter has passed, after his ex-wife has remarried, after you've both stopped grieving your dog. All his drunken posting, all his drunken falls. The helplessness. The many sleeping pills. The vomit you clean up. And the years that go by, oh, how the years go by.

Your love, a trap door under a trap door under a trap door. Your hands unpacking all the years now gone. The tablecloth, an endless plastic desert. The sigh you breathe before you begin. And here they go: all things lost, forgotten, meant but never done, offered but not taken. The tasteless gluten cloud he likes. And the beer, always the beer, oh so much beer, great men need to conquer their cosmoses of beer.

The chives, the peppermint, the beetroot. That glitch in your heart that makes you always stay, never leave. The mezzanine on which you fucked that other boy, all breathless, with oh-so-bright down covering his calves and oh-so-bright teeth. The January day when your so-called love walked in on the two of you: a professor and her student, half her age. He stopped in the doorway, blinking, then slowly turned away, his rods and cones clearly dying to see more, and never mentioned it later.

The pills you keep popping. A handful, a roomful. The pomegranate juice you like with your beer. The brown sugar. The lemons. *Just wait*, you keep telling yourself, after his funeral, after you've stopped grieving. After all things have been sorted out. After he's been dead for ten years, twenty years, fifty. After professors stop seducing their students and labs are only places to dissect the world. After all shopping bags are unpacked, all beer bottles empty.

Hydrogen and Diamonds

If packed tight enough, Neptune could hold 58 Earths.

*

Neptune was named after the Roman god of the sea, a rip-off of the Greek Poseidon.

*

Like its near-twin Uranus, Neptune owes its blue tint to methane. Neptune's blue is deeper though, gloomier, reminiscent of the ocean.

*

The atmosphere of Neptune is roughly eight parts hydrogen, two parts helium with traces of methane. The hydrogen could send 2 billion Hindenburgs into the air. The helium would suffice to blow up 15 quadrillion balloons. The methane wouldn't be enough to warm my frigid heart before I met you.

*

Neptune is the only planet in the solar system that can't be seen with the naked eye.

*

Your eyes looked like Great Dark Spots when you talked to me about Neptune. I fed you sunflower seeds under the cloudless sky, ran my fingers through your beard as your foot moved across the blanket and up my hairy calf.

*

One Neptunian year ago, Baudelaire published *The Flowers of Evil*. It's been
a whole Neptunian century since we ventured into European steppes in
search for a better life. Some 400 Neptunian millennia before that, an aged
sauropod craned its long neck towards the flaming sky.

*

Neptune's heart is mostly ices and rock, ices being what smart people call
water, ammonia, methane, and the like. I wasn't as smart when I told you
I needed more time, it was too soon after my last breakup, I was too much
of a mess. Thankfully, you were smart enough to wait.

*

You named Neptune's five feeble rings, then said how noise overwhelmed
you, how you hated crowds. I suggested we get out of here, move
somewhere quieter, emptier, less queerphobic. You didn't want to hear
about it, reminded me this was our home.

*

Neptune could hold nearly 3.5 billion Black Seas.

*

We planned to hang a photo of Neptune above our bed after we moved
in together. You hoped hundreds of hours spent on that coding bootcamp
would pay off. I wanted to ditch my job that was killing me and get serious
about my music.

*

It takes sunlight a good four hours to reach Neptune.

*

You bounced on that yoga ball like on a little Neptune all day, the monitor
painting your face blue. You said it calmed you down, helped you focus.
Plus, it was a good way to burn off some of that beer.

*

Neptune could hold 18 trillion of your dusty, cramped flats where
we kissed for the first time after your birthday party under a cobalt
sky of balloons.

*

Neptune couldn't hold your grief when your brother got killed.

*

It's possible Neptune's methane gets squashed into diamonds
that constantly rain towards the planet's core until they
evaporate.

*

Winds on Neptune almost reach supersonic speeds. It's only 16 times faster than my car when I drove to your place after I heard the news.

*

Like Uranus, Neptune likely formed closer to the sun but moved further away into the lifeless void.

*

The layered interior of Neptune reminds me of how I tried to peel you like an onion, but you kept slipping out of my hands. It was a chilly afternoon in the middle of winter, in the middle of nowhere. And by nowhere, I mean what was left of my home town after the bombs fell.

*

Neptune doesn't fuck around with its surroundings. Its strong gravitational pull sends Kuiper's belt bodies on some precarious orbits.

*

We tried to get out, but it was too late. Dragging suitcases across frozen fields, you bombarded me with trivia about Neptune. We heard the barking, the gunshots.

*

Neptune has 14 known moons. The largest moon, Triton, was once a planet of its own before it got caught in the invisible snare where it stayed, going round and round in a retrograde orbit, its surface frozen, its core quenched.

*

It's raining diamonds in Neptune's depths as we huddle in the crowded shelter listening to the noisy sky.

Treasures

She calls us her little treasures. Her hair smells of the bonfire. We watch the star-studded sky with our sharp-sighted eyes, touch the cool grass. Just my little brother L and me, that is. K, the beautiful accident, won't happen for many years.

Dad, his black moustache even blacker in the dark, takes a stick to retrieve another potato from the cinders. Mum helps us remove the coal-flavoured crust to reveal the fluffy interior.

From a pile of old planks, through the deafening chirping of crickets filling the garden, we hear the squeals of rats dying from poi—

—nting to a piece of paper on a crayon-littered floor, K shows me a planet populated by birds. Her curls remind me of DNA helices. Earlier that day, she exhumed her beheaded doll and reburied it under the willow. I wonder if plastic can turn into a fossil.

I am twenty-three, I listen to death metal, and my hair is dyed ruby red and woven into plaits. This evening—after a seemingly trivial conversation—Dad will call me a monster. When he gives us a lift to the station tomorrow morning, he'll know he messed up, but he'll be too proud to say 'I'm sorry.'

For now, though, the sun is setting and I'm looking outside the window at what remains of the family barbeque. On plastic chairs facing the enormous roses, Mum is talking to L. She's doing her best to make him come out to her. The harder she tries, however, the more he resembles an eel wriggling himself out of her hands. He'll never tell them the tr—

—easures can be found in unexpected places. K, a sad plump child one second ago, is now a slender woman in her twenties, lining the living-room carpet with L's childhood drawings. A series of Smurfettes in the sea, all scribbled with a blue ballpoint pen and posed like *The Birth of Venus*, waves on top of waves on top of waves in the background.

We're having a blast, forgetting for an instant about K's university across the continent, L's alcoholic boyfriend of twelve years, the rented flat I share with my loving, if slightly bossy, husband.

Mum is not in the scene. She must be vacuuming or washing dishes or shopping or crying silently in the corner. Dad, his moustache now silver, watches us from across the room. He doesn't say a word, but he beams with pr—

—ancing about the TV screen, sporting feathery gowns and fluttering lashes, drag queens put on their best show but no one's really watching. Mum seems to be counting needles on the Christmas tree with K's head resting on her shoulder. L is texting the doctor. I'm sitting with Dad's laptop on my lap, staring into *Things to deal with after.docx*.

Dad is now so small, but he seems to fill the entire house. From my parents' bedroom where he's lying, he seeps into the vestibule, then branches out to the corridor, bathroom, K's bedroom, living room, kitchen over the stairs to the remaining bedrooms and the attic filled with dusty furniture, unhung doors, bags of toys that haven't been touched in decades.

The tumours have it nice and cosy in his belly, collecting all the treasures: carbohydrates, proteins, and fats, vitamins and oxygen, minerals and metals, drinking blood like a smoothie. The fluid in his bag has turned brown. We fear his colon might have burst, letting out fe—

—athers pirouette in the air and fall onto glittery waves. I've been dead for millions of years. Birds have taken over the planet, occupying all the ecological niches. There are flying birds, swimming birds, slithering birds, birds the size of mammoths and as small as insects, birds that spend their entire lives in the clouds and birds that live in the blood of other birds.

Where our house used to stand, there's a gigantic floating nest surrounded by a shallow sea. The beautiful monster of a bird that resides in it, rosettes of peacock-like feathers around its head and paws, lets out a rattling screech. It tilts its head, eyeing the twilit sky, the yellow swarms of mosquito-sized tits, the enormous water lilies that are home to fluorescent mushrooms.

Finally, after preening its feathers for a bit, it stretches its spine, clumsily crawls out of the nest and plunges underwater—where its grace is endless.

Acknowledgements

Thank you to Janae Mancheski for her loving, insightful edits and cover design, as well as Freddy La Force and the rest of VA Press for seeing something in my weird little collection.

Thank you to my dear writer friends Tara Isabel Zambrano, Cathy Ulrich, and Ross Showalter for reading *Riverine* ahead of publication and crafting beautiful blurbs.

Speaking of writer friends, thank you also to Meg Pillow, Pat Foran, Dan Crawley, Kim Magowan, Tommy Dean, Anna Vangala Jones, Kathy Fish, Shome Dasgupta, Amy Barnes, Sara Dobbie, Tara Stillions Whitehead, Hannah Grieco, Kristin Tenor, Anita Goveas, Robert Vaughan, Janice Leagra, and many more I'm inevitably forgetting to mention. I appreciate your ongoing support.

Thank you to Emily Nemchick for editing many of these pieces before I sent them out to the world.

Thank you to all my friends and loved ones who have supported me and my writing throughout the years: my dearest Mum and sisters Kasia and Karolina, Kacper, Edi, Ewa P., Gaja and Łukasz, Gosia and Ewa F., Kasia Ł., Ola, Piotr, Justyna, Wiktor, Agi — the list could go on.

Last but not least, thank you to all the editors who gave many *Riverine* pieces lovely homes before they were assembled into a book.

'Cetacean' was first published in 2018 in *Quarterly West*. 'Moths' was first published in 2015 in *Lighthouse*.

'Devonian' was first published in 2018 in *The Gravity of the Thing*.

'Cellulose' was first published in 2018 in *Mojave Heart Review* (defunct) and then republished in 2020 in *FlashFlood*.

'Elements' was first published in 2018 in *The Chaffin Journal*.

'Drones' was first published in 2017 in *Bare Fiction*.

'Nameless' was first published in 2020 on *Akashic Books* website.

'Deadlines' was first published in 2020 in *STORGY*.

'Airborne' was first published in 2019 in *Transformation Anthology (The Selkie)*.

'Spores' was first published in 2019 in *X-R-A-Y Literary Magazine*.

'Landmines' was first published in 2019 in *Foglifter*.

'Entrails' was first published in 2019 in *Pithead Chapel*.

'Coal and Glitter' was first published in 2020 in *HAD* and then republished in 2023 in *Get Bent (Bending Genres)*.

'Phagocytosis' was first published in 2022 in *Stranged Writing: A Literary Taxonomy (The Gravity of the Thing)*.

'Riverweed' was first published in 2020 in *BULL*.

'Echoes' was first published in 2020 in *Fractured Lit*.

'Vacuoles' was first published in 2022 in *Split Lip Magazine*.

'Treasures' was first published in 2019 in *Atticus Review*.